# The Noah's Ark Adventure

Written by E M Wilkie

Illustrated by E M Wilkie

**The author would like to acknowledge the very helpful Noah's Ark pamphlet produced by Rose Publishing on which some of the illustrations in this book are based.**

Published by Indie Christian Book Group

an imprint of Indiego Publishing LLC

United States of America

www.indiego-epublishing.com

Print book ISBN: 978-0-9887048-3-1

It all began one rainy day,

When Emily had come to stay

With her four favourite cousins who

Always found lots of things to do!

But on one wet and stormy day—

Where should they go? What should they play?

And then Zach thought he had a plan—

And so adventure now began...

With toys enough for everyone

They played and laughed, and had such fun

Pretending they were all at sea

When all at once, quite suddenly...

Of Emily they saw no sign—
She'd gone, and left them all behind!
She'd got inside the ark somehow;
So what on earth should they do now?

Now Harry knew that only he

Was small enough to look and see

Inside the ark where she had gone—

But then another thing went wrong...

He vanished just as she had done!

Something quite funny had begun

And Zach and Seth and Bobs now thought

That since they'd gone they really ought

To see if they could follow too—

They did not know what else to do!

They lay down flat upon the floor

And peered in through the little door,

Then in an instant they were through

And met up with the other two—

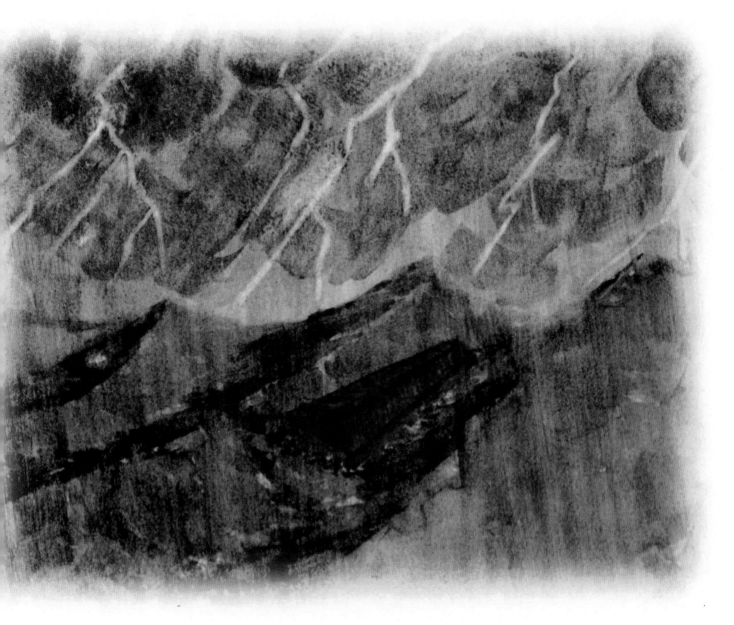

Inside a great big wooden boat

Which swayed and tossed and was afloat!

On Noah's ark they knew they stood,
Three storeys high, of gopher wood.

It was three hundred cubits long

And fifty wide, and very strong!

**With pitch to make it watertight—**

**All God's design, which made it right.**

One window only, just one door—
God shut it tightly to make sure
One family would be safe inside
When all the rest of mankind died.

There was a pair of every beast,

And of the clean ones, "Seven at least,"

Said Seth, "and Harry look right there—

A Daddy and a Mummy bear!"

And lions, monkeys, cows and hogs,

And elephants and friendly dogs,

And camels, horses, sheep and cats,

And penguins, birds and hanging bats,

Squirrels, mice and even moles—

Who had some soil to dig some holes—

For that great flood was all around

And came up even from the ground!

Giraffes and rabbits, kangaroos,

Caterpillars, ants and shrews,

Snails and spiders, even bugs

And centipedes and slimy slugs;

To every creature God was kind:

He had not left one type behind.

But if God took such tender care

To bring the creatures safely there—

"Where are the people?" Bobby thought,

He knew that God would want them brought

Into the ark before the seas

Would overwhelm His enemies.

And thus, since God had longed to show

His love for men on earth below,

He'd made a way by which they could

Be safe from judgement if they would.

So Noah preached for many days,

And spoke of God's unbounded grace

If only they would get inside

The ark, and from God's judgement hide;

But sadly they had all ignored

The warnings of God's holy Word.

And so it was, on that last day,

That only Noah's family

Would go into the ark before

It was too late—God shut the door.

For forty days the waters rose

As awful judgement fell on those

Who had despised the love of God—

They perished in a dreadful flood.

And hills and mountains, moor and heath,

And men and beasts were all beneath

Some seven metres height of flood

Which nothing there could rise above.

One day the ark came to a stop

And rested on a mountain top.

Then Noah sent a dove to see
If land was now from water free;
The first time it could find no rest
Outside the ark to make a nest.

The second time a leaf it bore—

The flood was getting less, for sure:

For God had made a wind to blow

And now the waters were brought low.

**Five months the ark of Noah sat**

**Upon the top of Ararat.**

Until at last there came a day
When God told all the family:
"It's safe for you to leave the ark,
Now everything can disembark."

So Noah and his sons obeyed

And did what God in heaven said;

An altar they designed and made

And on it offerings they laid.

And when God saw the sacrifice

He said, "I won't bring water twice,

I'll never flood the earth again—

In mercy I will deal with men:

And, as a token for you, I

Will place a rainbow in the sky."

Now although God has
promised men
To never flood the earth
again,
He must still punish all
the wrong
That everyone on earth
has done.

And like the ark, God made a way

To keep us safe eternally:

To save us from sin's punishment

The Lord Jesus to earth was sent,

And if we simply trust in Him,

He'll save us from God's wrath at sin.

Then suddenly, they knew not how,

They were no longer there, but now

They all sat on Seth's little bed,

Though how they got there, who had led

Them out of Noah's ark again

They really could not quite explain!

And then they noticed
at the door

Their mummies, who
said, "There you are—

The rain has stopped,
and just outside

There is a rainbow
high and wide!"

"Put on your welly boots and macs

And in the garden at the back

Go out and play and get fresh air,

You must be glad to be out there!"

"And let's see if you think you know

Why God made that first great rainbow...?"

Made in the USA
Charleston, SC
20 September 2014